Planet Kay

The Fly

A Black Hole

The Space Giant's
Beanstalk

Oddball

Major Tom

Adventures of Major Tom
The Space Pirates

written and illustrated by PETER LONGDEN

Ladybird Books Loughborough

The flying orange was speeding through the galaxy. At the controls was Major Tom and his robot assistant, Oddball. They were on one of their monthly space patrols.

Suddenly the interspace telephone buzzed. This kept them in touch with all the planets in space, and Oddball rushed to answer.

"It's base control," he shouted.

"I'll take it," replied Tom. "Major Tom here, sir. Can I help?"

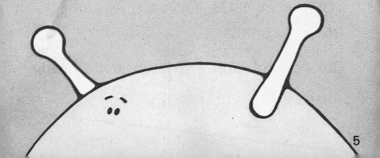

Tom's instructions from base control were short.

SET AN URGENT COURSE FOR THE PLANET KAYTERUS . . . ON ARRIVAL AT THE PLANET A SHUTTLE CRAFT ESCORT WILL BE PROVIDED . . . IT WILL TAKE YOU TO A SAFE LANDING PLACE ON THE SURFACE.

But control didn't say what the problem was.

Tom set a course for Kayterus and then switched to auto pilot. He left Oddball to tell him when they made contact with the planet.

As they approached Kayterus the radar bleeped. Oddball turned on the televiewer and saw what he thought must be the space shuttle. But he wasn't sure!

Oddball told Major Tom, who soon joined him in the control room. Putting the orange into manual control, they followed the strange little craft at a safe distance. It led them down to the surface of Kayterus.

As they stepped out on to the planet, they were greeted by a friendly robot.

"I'm Sheff, Cakemaster General," he said in a mechanical voice.

"Pleased to meet you," said Tom.

"You can see," went on Sheff, pointing to the Cakefields around them, "we grow every kind of delicious cake here, and we send them all over the solar system." Tom and Oddball looked.

They couldn't believe their eyes when Sheff showed them round the Cakefields, which were bursting with cakes of every shape and size.

Green and yellow robots were busy working in the fields, collecting the mouth-watering harvest.

One of the yellow robots invited them to taste some of the many delicious cakes.

Tom picked a cream delight, while Oddball tasted a cherry surprise.

Looking at all the goodies, Tom was wondering what problems a planet like this could have.

"I wish all our missions were as good as this," he mumbled between mouthfuls. "Can you tell me what's wrong?"

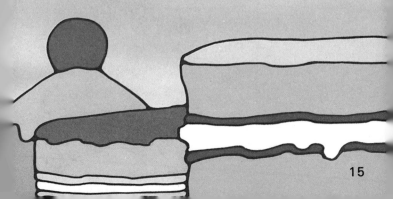

As Tom finished off his second cream cake, they were joined by another robot who was looking very worried.

He was the chief robot, who was in charge of delivering the cakes safely to their customers all over the galaxy.

"For years we have given a good service, and now suddenly our ships are being attacked," he said.

"Attacked?" questioned Tom.

"Yes," replied the robot. "There is a wicked space pirate called Captain Kid who is attacking our ships and stealing our cakes. We don't know how to stop him and we shall lose all our customers if we can't deliver their cakes."

Tom listened as the first robot came back and carried on the story.

"The pirates use all kinds of tricks to send our ships off course, then they swoop down in their space sailing-craft and steal the cakes. They are selling them to other planets for huge profits! Please can you help us?"

Tom decided that he must get rid of this crook at once and he and Oddball set off for the pirate's planet.

On the way they had a narrow escape when the star highwayman started shooting at the flying orange.

''This doesn't seem to be a very safe part of the galaxy,'' muttered Oddball.

As the flying orange got nearer to the pirate's planet, Captain Kid received a message from one of his satellites, warning him of the approaching space ship.

"Look lively there!" shouted Captain Kid. "There's an orange on its way and I don't remember inviting it!"

The pirates scrambled aboard their flying vessel.

"Cast off," boomed the captain, "and set full sail."

"Aye, aye, Captain!" replied the mate. The boat sped through the water until it reached take-off speed, then quickly rose into the air.

"Check the cannon," shouted Captain Kid. "We'll force the orange down on to the planet and take a look inside. Then we'll see what treasure it carries. Ha! Ha! Ha!"

Tom and Oddball were not ready for the attack by the pirates.

The cannon boomed and only just missed them. The orange shook and began to spin wildly. Then it began to fall, faster and faster. It was out of control.

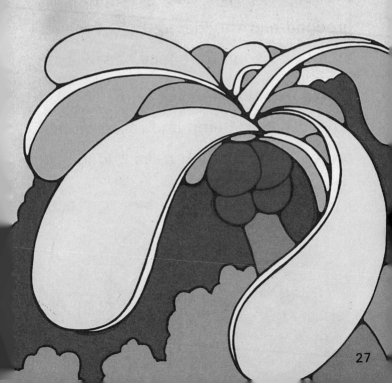

Oddball wrestled with the controls as they hurtled towards the planet's surface.

"Reverse power!" shouted Tom. "Or we shall crash."

With one last great effort Oddball pushed the power lever. The orange groaned and shuddered, but at the last minute it began to reduce speed.

"Hold on tight!" yelled Tom. They landed with a bump and rolled on and on, crashing through trees and jungle undergrowth.

29

Tom and Oddball helped each other to climb out of the orange. They were bruised and dizzy but unhurt. More important was the fact that they could hear the pirates searching for the orange.

"Hide in the jungle," shouted Oddball, dashing ahead. But when he stopped for a rest, he turned back just in time to see Tom disappearing down a hole in the ground. The pirates were too close for Oddball to try and rescue Tom.

Tom shot down to the bottom of the hole. It was dark and damp. The sides were steep and all he could see was the sky. Escape was impossible.

Suddenly, Tom heard voices . . . the pirates were closing in!

A shadow passed across the top of the hole and, as Tom looked up, a beady eye stared at him. It was Captain Kid.

"Pull that stupid space cat out," he snarled. "Tonight he can walk the plank."

Tom was roughly dragged out of the hole. He wondered what had happened to Oddball because he was sure that he wouldn't enjoy walking the plank — whatever that was!

The pirates took Tom away.

Oddball had been watching.
He knew what walking the plank
was and he knew he had to try
and rescue Major Tom.

Tom was bundled aboard the pirate's ship, and it took off again out into space. Then Tom was blind-folded and pushed along the plank.

''Here's a light so that you can see where you're going!'' scoffed Captain Kid, and with a quick prod he sent Tom falling through space. Down and down went Tom with the sound of Captain Kid laughing high above him.

All this time Oddball had been busy. He had returned to the orange and launched Segment One, the high speed mini-ship. He had followed the pirates and just as Tom was thinking this was his end, Oddball flew in and gave Tom a soft landing.

Returning to the planet Tom and Oddball plunged into the jungle in search of the pirates' hideout.

"We may be outnumbered," purred Tom, "but never outwitted."

After searching for some time they suddenly saw the pirates' flag, the Jolly Roger, flying from their fortress.

"Come on, Oddball," said Tom. "We've got them this time."

Unknown to them however they had been spotted. "They've walked right into our hands once more, lads!" laughed Captain Kid.

But the pirates didn't realise that something else was watching all of *them*.

It was the deadly candy-striped python. The pirates ran for their lives, but Captain Kid couldn't run because of his wooden leg.

The python came towards the Captain. He shook with terror, but he could not move as the python wound itself round and round him.

Tom and Oddball crept through the undergrowth to see what all the noise was about. The python's grip was slowly tightening, and it smiled at the thought of its dinner.

"Quick!" said Tom. "We must help him."

"Leave it to me," shouted Oddball, springing into action.

Then with one mighty blow to the head, he stunned the deadly snake and it slowly let go of the Captain.

Oddball quickly leapt in and soon had the python tied up in knots.

48

"You saved my life," said a grateful Captain Kid. "How can I repay you?"

"How about giving up space crime for ever?" Tom said quietly.

The Captain frowned. "That's all very well, but what are we going to live on?"

"Why not join the Space Federation as a special agent?" suggested Tom.

"And help us to make the galaxy a happier place!" added Oddball.

"Shiver me timbers! What a good idea," exclaimed the Captain. "I think I'd like being a special agent."

So Major Tom made Captain Kid take the oath to right all wrongs in space and never to misbehave again. Then Tom and Oddball took off in the orange.

Once in space Oddball said, "Another successful mission."

Tom wrinkled up his nose. "And one less villain to have to fight in the future."

SS Moon Cheese

Pisces

Little Bear

A Magnetic Field

Great Bear